Pond
Babies

Cathryn Falwell

Down East

ISBN 978-0-89272-920-3

Designed by Lynda Chilton

Printed in Singapore

5   4   3   2   1

Library of Congress Cataloging-in-Publication Data

Falwell, Cathryn.
  Pond babies / by Cathryn Falwell.
    p. cm.
  Summary: Examines some of the different animal
babies at the pond, such as a duck, a turtle, and a
loon. Includes note to parents on what to do at a
pond.
  ISBN 978-0-89272-920-3 (trade hardcover : alk.
paper)
 [1. Pond animals--Fiction. 2. Animals--Infancy--
Fiction. 3. Ponds--Fiction.] I. Title.
 PZ7.F198Po 2011
 [E]--dc22
                                    2010043117

Down East
BOOKS·MAGAZINE·ONLINE
www.downeast.com

Distributed to the trade by National Book Network

For Nancy Craig

Will we
see babies
down at
the pond?

This baby has a  **striped** face.

Whose baby is this?

Duck's baby.

This baby has a

shell for hiding.

Whose baby is this?

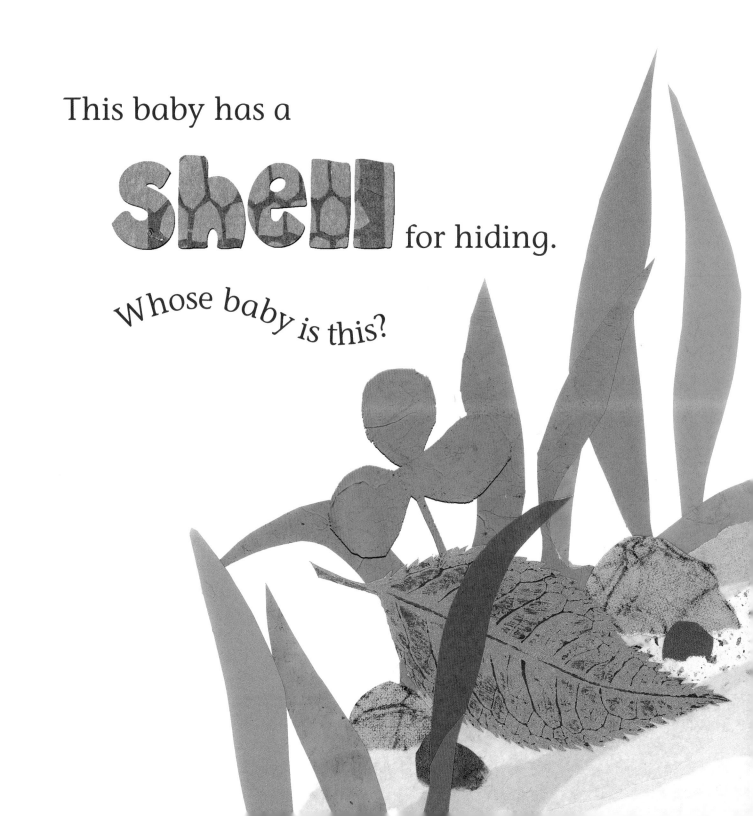

Turtle's baby.

This baby has a wiggly tail.

Whose baby is this?

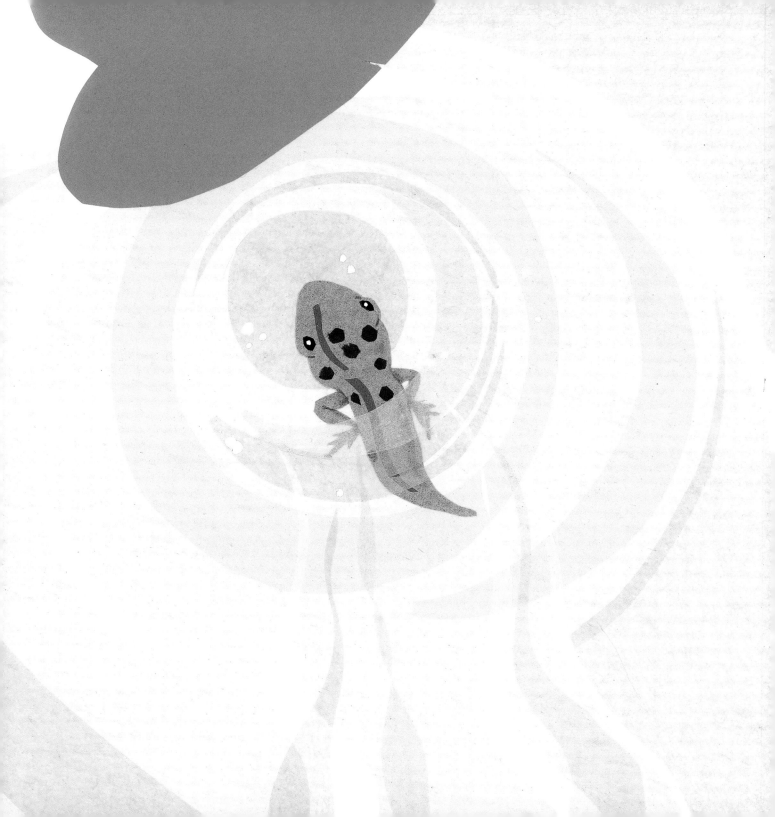

Frog's baby.

This baby has many **white spots.**

Whose baby is this?

Deer's baby.

This baby has

fluffy feathers.

Whose baby is this?

Loon's baby.

This baby has  toes.

Whose baby is this?

MY baby!

Be a Pond Baby!

Can you...

...waddle and quack

...wiggle like a tadpole?

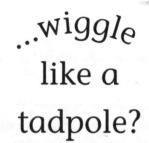

like a duckling?

...hide like a turtle hatchling?

..run like a fawn?

...*dive* and POP ^{UP} like a loon chick?

Go Outside and Play!

It's fun to explore the natural world with your child. Whether you live in the city or the country, you can always find ways to interact with nature. Encourage your child's curiosity and sense of wonder, while gently providing safety and guidance. Pause to look up at the sky or turn over a rock. This will make your child more curious about the world around them. Let your senses guide your discoveries:

SEE

In addition to pond babies and other critters, the great outdoors is a wonderful place to look for colors and shapes Look at a tree together and talk about how many colors you see. Look at the clouds or the rocks at your feet to find new shapes.

HEAR

Find a quiet place where you and your child can listen to nature: the wind in the leaves; the singing of crickets, birds, or frogs; the sound of water.

TOUCH

Stones, shells, twigs, and tree bark are tactile delights for young children. Most plants, too, are safe to gently touch. Little hands can always be washed later.

SMELL

Encourage your child to sniff the flowers, as well as tree trunks, rocks, and other interesting things they discover.

TASTE

Unless you really know about wild berries and other edible plants, bring along a healthy snack on outdoor outings.

Prepare for nature adventures with sunscreen and protective clothing. Help your child respect and love their natural environment, and be sure to have fun!